Forest of Doom

Forest of Doom has been
specially commissioned
for Tesco.

COVER ILLUSTRATION *Sam Hadley*

Published for
Tesco Stores Limited
by Brilliant Books Ltd
84-86 Regent Street
London W1R 6DD

First published 1998

Printed by Redwood Books, England
Reproduction by Colourpath, England

Forest of Doom

Jennie Walters

TESCO

CHAPTER ONE

Mel stared ahead into the wood. Where was that stupid brother of hers? There was no sign of him, and they should be getting back to the car park. She knew it had been a mistake to let Tom go off on a different path.

"We'll meet you at the car," her mother had said, when Tom had wanted to shoot ahead. "Keep an eye on him, won't you, Mel?"

She'd been hearing those words ever since she could remember. Why should she have to look after her idiot younger brother all the time? Why couldn't she sometimes just do what *she* wanted?

"But it's my *birthday*, Mum," she'd argued. "I don't want to go with him. I want to go home and start getting my bedroom ready for tonight."

Her best friends, Claire and Ashley, were coming for a sleepover party. They were going to toast marshmallows, make popcorn, and watch the videos that Mel had spent hours choosing.

"Now look, Mel," her mother began, "just go with Tom and make sure he doesn't get lost. We'll meet you in the car park. You'll have plenty of time to enjoy yourself later. You can spare him ten minutes now."

"You know where the car is, don't you?" her father had added. "Just beyond that clump of trees at the top of the hill."

"Yes, Dad, of course I do," Mel had flung grumpily back over her shoulder.

Though now she was beginning to doubt her sense of direction.

In summer, the forest trees grew so thickly together that the sunlight turned to greeny-gold as it trickled down through a filter of leaves.

But now only the dark pines showed any sign of green, and the sun had long since disappeared. Mel shivered in her thin sweatshirt. She loved Coldharbour Woods – that was why she'd chosen to come here as part of her birthday treat. But now she'd had enough. She wanted to get home and make sure everything was perfect before Claire and Ashley came.

Oh, where was that stupid boy? Mel peered into the trees on each side of the winding path. Coldharbour Woods were huge, stretching on for miles around, but people only walked on the outskirts. A few wide paths had been cleared and given names, like The Sika Trail and The Silver Birch Walk. Some narrower tracks had been carved out over the years as people took shortcuts. Tom had gone off on one of these, and he seemed to have vanished into thin air.

"Tom!" Mel called yet again.

She listened for a reply, but none came. The only sounds were the rustling of dead leaves on the ground, and now and then the harsh cawing of rooks. Mel shivered again and glanced nervously behind her. She couldn't shake off the feeling that someone was watching her, and it made her heart thump in her chest. She had to admit that she was beginning to get frightened, out here in the woods on her own. Why weren't there a few more people around? There'd been loads of families when they started their walk.

Mel jumped as a twig cracked loudly nearby. A cold hand of fear clutched at her stomach. She whirled around, her eyes darting from tree

to tree, trying to see something – anything –
only to be met by a thick wall of branches.

And then she saw him.

Tom was propped up against a tree trunk at
the side of the track. His head was on one side,
blond hair flopping over his face. Strange, half-
strangled noises were coming out of his mouth.

And a hand was around his neck, the fingers
pressing hard against his throat.

CHAPTER TWO

"Tom!" Mel screamed, rushing forward. "Hang on. I'm coming!"

She ran towards her brother, her eyes fixed on his slumped body, her heart pounding and her brain frozen in panic. All she could think of was how to get to him as quickly as possible. She didn't stop to ask herself who – or what – might be attacking him.

Tom's eyes were rolling now, turning up so that she could see the whites.

"Let him go!" she screamed. "I'll kill you!"

She had almost reached Tom when he jumped out on to the path in front of her.

"Ha ha! Fooled you," he sang. He danced off with one arm twisted up behind his back and around his neck. "Let him go! I'll kill you!" he mimicked, laughing fit to burst. Then he started making gagging noises again, and staggering from side to side.

"You idiot!" Mel shouted in fury. What did he think he was doing, giving her a fright like that? She was extra angry now. She felt like killing Tom, he was always such a pain in the neck. How would he like it if she pulled a trick like that on him?

If only people could see what her brother was really like. He was always winding her up, and she was the one who got the blame when she lost her temper. He was definitely her parents' favourite. Grown-ups all thought Tom was funny and cute.

"Look at that hair," they'd say. "And those eyes! Eyelashes like that are wasted on a boy."

Then they'd turn and look at Mel, and they wouldn't say anything else.

It wasn't fair, Mel thought bitterly. Tom could get away with anything. She was just the mousy older sister when he was around. No one ever took any notice of a tall girl with messy brown hair.

"Cheer up, Mel," her grandmother used to say. "Tom'll lose his pretty baby face, then you'll be the one with all the admirers. And those lovely green eyes of yours, Mel! You have the seeing eyes." And she would nod her head.

'The seeing eyes'? What's that supposed to mean? Mel wondered to herself.

Gran often came out with funny little sayings like that. "I understand things. It's on account of my Romany blood," she would say. "There's a gypsy side to the family, you know."

But Mel's mother just laughed and said it was more likely on account of Gran having been at the cooking sherry. And when she died, there were no gypsy caravans at the funeral – much to Mel's disappointment.

Perhaps 'the seeing eyes' were something to do with Mel having been born on All Hallow's Eve. Hallowe'en, when witches and warlocks swoop through the sky! Her grandmother once told her that people born then had the gift of second sight. They could see things hidden to ordinary people.

Mel had felt quite special for a while, but she soon forgot about it. She couldn't predict the winning Lottery numbers, after all.

And just now, she couldn't even seem to find

her way home. Oh, why couldn't they only get back on the right path and out of here? This birthday walk was turning into a nightmare.

She ran to catch up with Tom and grabbed his arm. "Look, stay with me till we get to the car," she ordered.

He'd given her a bad shock, and her heart was still pounding. She just wanted to be back where everything was safe and familiar. In the car with her mum and dad or – even better – at home with her friends.

It was cold and forbidding in this lonely part of the wood. The walks they usually took were among the pines that had been recently planted. But here, they had stumbled across a part of the wood which seemed to be older. All the trees were so gnarled and enormous. Mel didn't know that much about trees, but she could recognise the huge oaks from the shape of their trunks, and elms too. They must have been here for years.

Tall trees loomed over the path. Mel stared up at their spiky branches, stabbing the autumn sky. They look like fingers, she thought. Long, bony, skeleton fingers. And when the breeze stirred them, they scraped together with a dry whisper. "Go away," they seemed to be murmuring. "Go home."

Oh, come on, she said to herself. You're just imagining things. We'll soon get to the car, and everything will be fine.

But as it turned out, they didn't.

And it wasn't.

CHAPTER THREE

"Admit it, Mel – we're lost, aren't we?"

Tom glared at his sister. He wasn't in the mood for playing tricks on her now. Then he turned his back and started kicking at a tree stump. "Why can't you just say you don't know where the car is? We've been going round in a circle for at least the last half hour."

He wasn't looking at Mel, but she knew he was close to tears. And that made her feel even worse.

"Oh, stop making such a fuss," she replied. "We'll get back on the right path sooner or later. We'll probably walk straight into Mum and Dad, looking for us."

But Mel wasn't fooling anyone, not even herself.

She tried to control the panic that was making her voice tremble. What was happening? Where had they gone wrong? She thought she knew the wood like the back of her hand. But the two of them had been wandering around for ages without coming across anything she recognised.

They seemed to be heading deeper into the heart of the forest, and it was not the forest Mel knew. Everything was so quiet, and still. The distant sounds of other ramblers had faded away and their own noisy footsteps seemed even louder in the eerie silence.

"I'm cold, Mel," Tom grumbled.

"Well, you're not the only one," she muttered, rubbing the goosebumps on her arms.

"Why did you say you knew the way to the car when you don't?" Tom accused her bitterly. "We're lost and it's all your fault!"

"My fault!" Mel snapped back at him. "Whose idea was it to run off ahead in the first place? Don't forget, it's my birthday as well! How do you think I'm feeling? Why don't you ever think about someone else apart from yourself for a change?"

Tom looked at her without speaking. His big dark eyes welled with tears and his narrow shoulders were hunched around his neck. Poor kid, Mel thought, softening. He's terrified.

"Come on," she said, trying to jolly him along. "Let's try calling again. There's bound to be somebody nearby."

Their shouts echoed around the quiet wood. Why couldn't anyone hear them? Where were their parents? It was as if they'd entered another world. An empty, hostile world where nature was not on their side. Sharp briars tore at their clothes and scratched their legs. Strangely shaped tree roots snaking along the ground tripped up their feet. Mel, who was in front, had to force her way through low, overhanging branches, which whipped back to slap Tom in the face.

She felt chilled to the bone. She peered ahead, a damp sweat of fear prickling its way along her spine. They were in real trouble, and no prizes for guessing who was in for a serious telling-off from Mum and Dad when they found them again. *If* they found them again.

She looked at the watch her parents had given her that morning. Its dayglo green numbers flashed out, but the time they told didn't make sense. It was exactly the same as when she'd last looked, which must have been at least fifteen minutes ago.

Great! Now even her present had broken. This was not going down in history as the best birthday she'd ever had.

"I'm tired. Can't we stop and have a rest?" Tom whined.

"No. We have to find the car before it gets dark." Mel tried to keep her voice light, but the thought of being out in this wood at night filled her with horror.

She rubbed her arms and shuddered. Dusk was falling already. The same raven seemed to have been cawing for the last ten minutes. The harsh ugly noise made her stretched nerves jangle. And that scraping, rustling sound from the trees was setting her teeth on edge. What were they trying to tell her?

Behind her, Tom was still grumbling. She could hear him muttering away to himself and slashing at the ferns with a stick. Then he called out, "Well, I'm not going any further till I've had a rest, whether you like it or not!"

"Oh for goodness' sake! Don't be so pathetic!" Mel shouted, turning to face her brother as he stood with his arms folded at the edge of the path.

And then she saw something that made her blood run cold.

A great branch of the tree behind Tom split away from the main trunk, with a loud crack like a gunshot. As if in slow motion, it started a steady fall to the ground, tearing away smaller branches and leaves as it went.

Gathering speed, faster and faster, down it crashed. Until it landed with a sickening, mighty thump. Directly on top of Tom.

CHAPTER FOUR

"But, Mel, how on earth did you know that tree branch was going to fall on me?" Tom asked, for the umpteenth time.

"I don't know. I just saw it in my head," Mel replied, yet again.

She couldn't explain why that picture had come into her head so terrifyingly clearly. Or how she'd known she had to dive forward in a long low rugby tackle and roll with Tom to one side of the path. She was just grateful she'd been in time.

Together, they stared at the huge, heavy bough. It had fallen with such force it was half-buried in the soft earth.

"It's an elm," Mel said. "Do you remember, Gran told us elm branches could break off with no warning? What was that rhyme she used to say? "'Elm hateth man, and waiteth.'"

She shuddered. This whole forest seemed to hate them. And just what was it waiting for?

"Come on," she said, getting shakily to her feet and pulling Tom up, too. "Let's get going."

Then she peered ahead into the gloom with sudden excitement. She had caught sight of a narrower track, branching off to the left ahead of them. Somehow, she had a strong feeling as though she'd been here before. Perhaps this was the right path at last!

Yes, there was that strange dead tree, with a huge hole in its trunk. It looked as though a twisted face with a wide-open mouth were trapped in the wood. Shouting at her.

Mel stumbled up to the tree and ran her hands over the rough bark. A couple of ants were scurrying into the dark hole at the centre of the knot. As she watched them, she saw a glint from deep within it. She carefully bent forward for a closer look, her excitement rising. There seemed to be something metal lying there. Could this secret hidey-hole have been chosen to store something precious? She was determined to find out.

Cautiously, Mel reached into the hollow, not

knowing what her searching fingers would meet. They touched a hard surface, smooth but shifting like a pile of tiny pebbles.

"Hang on a minute, Tom," she said over her shoulder. "I've found something!"

"I thought you were the one who wanted us to hurry up," he grumbled, sitting down again on a tree stump.

"This is important!" Mel answered, though she couldn't have said why. "It won't take long."

Slowly, she began to draw her fingers out, and found herself staring at a length of chain dangling between them. It was caught up inside the tree trunk, but patiently she worked away at untangling it. Gently does it, she told herself.

It was strange, but she had the distinct feeling that someone was watching her. As though eyes were boring into her back. But when she whirled around – there was no one there. Only the dark silent trees, looking down on her.

She went back to her task. At last, with one final tug, the chain was free.

Mel looked at it curiously. The links were thicker than she might have expected, and heavier, too. It was made to be worn, though.

An intricate clasp fastened the two ends together, and a short length of gold metal hung from a large central ring. Its bottom edge was jagged, as though it were part of a pendant which had been snapped off. Mel could just make out a few words engraved along it. It looked like Latin, but certainly nothing she could understand.

She held the chain up to the fading light, inspecting it closely. And then her ear caught a faint sound. Music was swelling up through the trees, carried through the rustling branches by the breeze. Deep voices were singing in harmony, so beautifully that Mel felt a shiver of delight run through her.

"Tom! Did you hear that?" she exclaimed, looking round.

But Tom had vanished.

CHAPTER FIVE

"Tom! Where are you?" called Mel.

She knew Tom wasn't likely to have pulled another trick on her. Not after what had just happened. So where was he? Someone must have snatched him, was all she could think. Her stomach lurched in panic and she felt sick with dread. Tom seemed to have been swallowed up by the wood. She was all alone in the middle of this grim, sinister place. The beautiful music had died away. And it was getting dark.

Mel stared frantically ahead into the soft autumn dusk, her heart racing. Her worst nightmare was coming true. She'd have no chance of finding Tom among the trees in the pitch dark. She'd never see him again. And she would be spending the night here, on her own.

She bolted down the path, the chain stuffed in

her pocket. The wind seemed to have sprung up, which made it even colder. And the trees were still rustling, murmuring together.

Wait a minute! What was that?

Mel strained her ears to catch a faint sound. She could hear people talking, she was sure of it. The noise seemed to be coming from behind that big sycamore. Leaving the path, she crashed through the undergrowth towards it, her hopes rising. Maybe someone had found Tom! At least they could show her which way to go.

"Help!" she cried, rushing forward. "Please help me!"

But as she reached the tree and then stumbled past it, she stared in dismay. The glade was empty. There was nobody there. She could have sworn...

And then she heard the voices again. They were coming from behind her now, and over to the right. Two or three people, she thought. No, more, it must be a crowd. Their voices rose and fell, talking all at the same time.

Now a low hum of sound seemed to be rising up out of the trees from every direction, echoing here, there and everywhere. The noise was inside her head and all around, confusing her senses and filling her with terror. She couldn't distinguish any words, but she caught the tone all right. It was unfriendly. Accusing. Menacing.

"Help!" she called again. Hopelessly this time, for she felt there was no human ear to hear her. Then, frantically, as the babble rose ever louder, she screamed, "Tom! Where are you?"

With that the meaningless string of words turned to mocking laughter. It rang down from every side, deafening her, flooding her head with awful sound.

"Leave me alone!" she shouted, holding her hands over her ears and stumbling on into the dusk. She crashed from tree to tree, sobbing with fear. Her clothes caught on branches and briars, as though pinching hands were tearing at her body. Wings seemed to be beating in her face and strands of hair were in her eyes, blinding her.

She would have run for ever in panic, had her feet not stumbled into something soft.

It was a body.

Tom's body.

CHAPTER SIX

Tom was lying huddled on the forest floor. His hands, too, were clasped tightly over his ears to shut out the explosion of sound that was still ringing through the trees. But he was alive, and conscious. When Mel tried to pull his hands away he resisted, struggling fiercely against her, kicking and lashing out.

"It's me, Tom," she shouted, half-lifting him off the ground. "Come on – we've got to get out of here. Now!"

She took his arm and together they ran back to the path, ducking under the terrifying uproar. They were rushing in blind panic, their feet crashing over leaves and mud, through puddles and ditches. Branches cracked beneath them, but they didn't care. There was no point in trying to hide from whoever or whatever was all around them.

And then, in the middle of their frantic journey, they felt the noise dying away. It seemed to be drawn back up into the trees, slowly becoming fainter and weaker. They could feel the voices behind them, rather than all around. They were escaping!

Eventually, when the pounding of their hearts and the stampede of their footsteps were the loudest sounds they could hear, they slowed down to a walk.

"I can't go any further," panted Tom, throwing himself down on the ground and fighting to get his breath back.

"What happened to you?" Mel asked him, when at last she could speak easily. "Why did you go off?"

"I heard people talking up ahead, so I went to find them," Tom replied. "Then the voices got louder and…"

"I know," Mel shuddered. She didn't want to remember what it had been like.

"There's something really weird going on here," Tom said. "We can't seem to get out of this place, and it's like somebody's… I don't know, somebody's playing games with us. What are we going to do, Mel?"

And as he looked up at her with big frightened eyes, Mel realised with horror that she really didn't know.

CHAPTER SEVEN

"We have to keep going," Mel told her brother. "There's nothing else we can do. We have to keep walking, and keep strong."

"But we've got no idea where we are," Tom said. "It feels like we're just getting more and more lost."

"I don't know," Mel replied. "You know when we stopped, back there? Well, I really felt like we'd found the right path, that I'd seen it before. And I still feel the same. I think we might be nearly there."

"Nearly where?" Tom asked. "Do you mean, nearly at the car?"

"No, not exactly. But nearly where we should be. Where the path is leading us."

"What are you talking about," Tom grumbled.

"I don't quite know myself," Mel confessed.

"I just think perhaps we're not all on our own here. You're right, something weird's going on, and we're caught in the middle. But maybe we've got some part to play in it all. Look, I found this chain in the tree."

And she fished it out of her pocket. The heavy links sparkled in the gloom and the chunk of gold gleamed. Without thinking what she was doing, she slipped it over her head and around her neck, where it nestled against her throat.

"Hey, that's stealing!" Tom accused her.

"I won't keep it," Mel replied. "I'm just going to borrow it for a while. Come on, let's get going. Why don't we sing something?"

That might help to keep our spirits up, she thought. And at least it'll stop us listening for voices in the dark.

They climbed wearily to their feet and set off once more through the trees, arms linked. Their voices rose into the evening air, sounding small and faint in the great dark forest. As soon as one song finished, they began another. Anything, rather than hear distant voices or mocking laughter from the shadows.

They'd run through a whole range of their favourites and Mel was just starting on 'All Things Bright and Beautiful' for the third time, when she clutched Tom's arm.

"Look!" she cried.

In front of them, half hidden in the shadows of night, stood a house. All on its own.

"Well?" said Tom. "Do you still think this is where we're meant to be?"

"I don't know," Mel answered doubtfully. The place seemed so lonely and deserted that her spirits sank just at the sight of it.

"Wow!" breathed Tom. "It looks like something out of a fairy story."

A thick creeper snaked its way up from a trunk beside the front door of the house to a tiny window just under the roof. Leaves covered every inch of the walls, twining around the window frames as though they were peering in.

"Perhaps this is where the forest ranger lives," Tom went on. "He'll be able to get us back to the car. I'm going to knock on the door and ask for help."

"Wait, Tom!" Mel told him. "We don't know who lives here. It could be some maniac! Mum's always telling us not to talk to strangers. Anyway, I don't think there's anyone home. The place looks deserted to me."

"There's a light on," Tom said, noticing a dim glow through half-drawn curtains at one of the downstairs windows. "And what else can we do? Nothing could be as bad as what's happened to us already. It's dark and we've got to get to somewhere safe. I can't stand it in this place!"

Before he could lose his nerve, he rushed up to the door and rapped on it loudly with the heavy knocker. The sharp sound echoed round the quiet clearing. A couple of rooks flew up from the trees, cawing loudly.

Mel caught her breath in alarm. It was too late now! They would soon find out who – or what – was living in that deserted-looking house. Slowly, she went up to join her brother on the doorstep. And as she did so, she caught sight of something that made her feel sure they were doing the wrong thing.

There, up at the attic window, was a flash of something white. It seemed to be floating in the air. But there was no time to run, because the door to the house was slowly creaking open.

CHAPTER EIGHT

The smell hit them first.

Mel and Tom gasped, and took a step backwards. What was it? A mixture of rotting leaves and damp grass, perhaps, with a splash of manure thrown in for good measure.

They were face to face with a woman. She had long straggly hair caught up in a bun, and she was wearing a black skirt that nearly touched the floor, and a baggy grey cardigan.

At the sight of the two children, her hand flew up to her mouth in horror.

"How did you get here? What's happened to you?" She stared at them in alarm with dark, deep-set eyes.

"We got lost in the wood," Tom said. "We thought there were people after us…" His voice trailed away. How could anyone possibly explain what they'd been through?

"We've got to get back to our parents," Mel explained. "They must be looking for us, and they'll be very worried. Perhaps you could ring the police, in case we've been reported missing?" she added.

The woman seemed to be hypnotised. She was just standing there, staring at them.

Finally, she murmured, "No, I can't do that. I don't have a phone, you see – it's too remote here. Come inside for a moment, and we'll think what to do."

No phone? Mel and Tom exchanged looks of disbelief. What kind of person could live without a telephone?

"We don't want to bother you," Mel said quickly. "Perhaps you could just take us to the main path so we can get back on our own."

There was no way she wanted to go inside the house. Every instinct, every nerve in her body screamed out against it. At least in the forest they were free – they could run if they had to. Something told her that once inside this house, it would be harder to escape.

"No, this is not a night to be out in Coldharbour Woods," replied the woman. She spoke quite firmly now, as though she had made up her mind about something. "And you're both in quite a state. Come in and I'll clean you up and give you something to eat and drink."

"Oh, all right then," said Tom, his eyes lighting up. He stepped over the threshold into the dim hallway of the house, as the woman stood back to let him pass.

"Tom!" Mel hissed desperately. She couldn't believe it! How could he walk into this stranger's house, just like that? Because he thinks of nothing but his stomach, of course, she answered herself.

And now it was too late to turn back. Tom was inside the house. The woman was looking at her expectantly, waiting for her to come in as well. She couldn't leave her brother there on his own.

Mel stepped forward, her legs trembling.

And then everything went black.

CHAPTER NINE

Mel opened her eyes. All she could see before them was a blue haze.

Then her head cleared and the haze swam into focus. It was her legs, propped up in front of her. She was sitting on the floor against a wall, with her head resting on her knees.

Slowly, she lifted her head. And gazed straight into the dark searching eyes of the woman who'd let them in. She gasped and looked around. Where was Tom?

"Gently, my dear," said the woman. "Just sit still for a few seconds."

"Are you all right, Mel?" came another voice. It was Tom, gazing down at her anxiously. "You gave us a real fright."

"I don't know what happened," Mel said. "I felt OK before. But then, as soon as I came in,

I got all dizzy, and…that's the last thing I remember."

"You fainted," said the woman. "I think it was just because you're tired, and your nerves are overstretched. Now, let's get you up at the table and you can have some herb tea." And she hauled Mel up to sit on a chair. She was surprisingly strong.

Mel took little sips from the steaming mug that was given her and looked around at the room she was sitting in. The smell that had hit them when the front door opened was even stronger here. It was like being back in the forest again, or some tropical jungle. There were plants everywhere. Dried flowers and herbs hung in bunches from beams across the low ceiling. Cuttings and seedlings crowded along every windowsill, and pots crammed full of spiky green shoots jostled for space on the uneven floor.

It was warm in the room, almost steamy. But despite the heat, Mel shivered. What were they doing here?

Desperation sounding in her voice, she said, "Please, please, can you just tell us how to get back to our parents? They must be somewhere nearby, and if we can only get back to the main path, I'm sure we'll find them."

"Now listen, my dear," said the woman, drawing nearer to Mel and looking at her closely, "this forest is not the place to be wandering around in the dark. And especially not tonight. You've found that out, haven't you? Tom has been telling me all about it."

Mel stared at her brother in alarm. What had Tom been saying? She felt strongly that the less this woman knew about them, the better.

"She knows about the voices, Mel. And I told her about the branch falling, and everything," Tom said eagerly. "Her name's Mrs Hardacre."

"Yes, Diana Hardacre," the woman added.

Mel struggled to her feet. "We have to go," she said. "You must have a neighbour, or some-body nearby with a phone, surely?"

"No," replied the woman, pushing her gently but firmly back down into the chair. "There's nobody around for miles. We're on our own."

The words struck horror into Mel's heart. They were trapped.

Mrs Hardacre went on, "Now listen to me.

Somehow, I don't know how, you and Tom have found a part of the woods where people don't usually come. It's a long way off the main path, and you'll only get yourselves into real trouble if you go out again tonight. You've had quite a scare already, and something even worse could happen."

"But what about our mum and dad?" Mel said urgently. "And all the people who are looking for us?"

"Oh, I don't think anybody's looking for you," said the woman. "But if they are, it would be better to stay here and wait to be found, wouldn't it?"

"People *are* looking for us, they must be!" Mel replied desperately. "I know we've been gone for ages."

"Well, I haven't heard anyone. Have you?" replied the woman. She looked at Mel, and smiled again. Triumphantly.

"I'll get you something to eat," she went on. "But first, you can clean yourselves up. Come through to the scullery." And she led them towards a door at the back of the kitchen.

Mel followed her into the room.

Then she screamed in terror and held up her arms to shield herself.

"Get away from me!" she yelled.

Wings were beating in Mel's face, and a harsh screeching rang in her ears, deafening her.

She was under attack again.

The evil, mocking horror from the woods had found her.

CHAPTER TEN

Once Mel had started screaming, she couldn't stop. The tiny space seemed to be full of people, full of noise. She tried to run, but which way to turn?

She was caught, there was no way out.

Then, through it all, she heard Tom's voice. "Don't worry, Mel," he was saying. "Calm down, it's all right."

Opening her eyes, she saw Diana Hardacre, with a large flapping bird, held tightly in her arms. "I forgot he was in here," she said. "I'll just put him in the shed." And she went out through the back door.

"Tom, we've got to get out of here," Mel gasped, when they were on their own. "This is an evil place."

"Get a grip, Mel," he said. "You've had a

fright, that's all. Don't get carried away!"

"I'm not imagining it," Mel told him."

But there was no time to say any more, for Mrs Hardacre was back in the house again. "That was an owl I found in the woods," she told Mel. "He'd hurt his foot, so I'm keeping him for a while. I'm sorry he gave you a fright."

And after that, Mrs Hardacre didn't leave them alone for a minute.

Mel couldn't believe how relaxed Tom was. She listened to him as she loosened her scrunchy hairband and shook her hair out of its ponytail. She brushed it, trying to calm her racing heart. Tom chattered about how spooky it had been in the forest. And it was Mel's birthday, too. She was meant to be having a sleepover party with her friends.

"Your birthday?" Mrs Hardacre said, glancing up at Mel sharply. "Well, indeed. All Hallow's Eve is a very special day to be born."

Mel looked away, feeling uncomfortable under that piercing stare. Why wouldn't Tom shut up? Couldn't he see how strange this was?

She gazed around the room. Everything seemed to be stored in earthenware pots or jugs, and it all looked home-made. A big old range stood in one corner of the room – that must be what was making it so hot.

Mel still felt dizzy, and faint. She was deeply uneasy. Something was wrong in this house, some great sense of sorrow hung over it. She could feel and almost touch it with her fingers.

Mrs Hardacre turned around from the iron range and returned Mel's look, as though she were answering a challenge. But all she said was, "Time to eat."

Mel was hungry, but the food looked like a science experiment gone wrong. There was a pile of dingy brown beans and an omelette, flecked with green herbs.

She began to nibble at some of the beans. She could feel Tom nudging her under the table, but when she looked across at him, he didn't lift his head from the plate. What was he trying to tell her?

Mel moved her leg away, but the pressure was still there. She put her hand down to investigate – and then felt her hair stand on end.

Something hairy was twining itself around her legs.

CHAPTER ELEVEN

"McCavity! Come out of there," scolded Mrs Hardacre.

The biggest black cat Mel had ever seen crept out from under the table. It stared at her silently for a moment with huge yellow eyes. Then, very deliberately, it turned its back and stalked out of the room.

"Well, you are jumpy, aren't you?" Mrs Hardacre said to Mel. "There aren't any more surprises, though. I promise you."

Tom threw his sister an 'I told you so' look, and Mel scowled back at him.

"You must be very tired," Mrs Hardacre said when the children had finished eating – or pretending to eat, in Mel's case. "I'll go and make up the beds in the spare room, then you can get some rest."

And with that, she went quietly out of the room, leaving the thick wooden door open behind her.

"Tom!" Mel hissed as soon as she thought there was no chance of being overheard. "How can you trust that woman? There's something really strange about her, and this house too. Why is she so keen for us to stay here? We don't know what she's planning!"

"Oh, get real, Mel," Tom answered. "What do you think she's going to do? Come and murder us in our beds? She's a bit weird, but I think she's OK."

"Well, I don't," Mel said definitely. "She's not making any effort to get help. She hasn't even bothered to look outside the door to see if anyone's searching for us."

"So what choice do we have?" Tom flung back at her. "We're lost, remember, and I wouldn't go back to those woods in the dark for a million pounds. We've got to stay, for the time being at least. We can leave in the morning. Mrs Hardacre can't keep us here against our will!"

Oh, can't she, Mel thought grimly. Something tells me she's going to try.

She bit her lip, trying not to cry. It was her birthday, and she was spending it in this strange house, instead of at home with her friends. She thought of her bright, happy room, covered wall to wall with posters. What wouldn't she give to be back there now!

Then she pictured her mother and father, searching and calling for them through the night. Her watch was still blinking out the same old flashing numbers, so she had no idea how late it was. But they must have been lost for a couple of hours, at least.

Why hadn't anyone come to find them? It was as if they'd both just vanished off the face of the earth.

"You can come upstairs now," said a voice behind her. Mel jumped, and turned around to see Mrs Hardacre standing in the doorway. How quietly she moved!

"The room is ready," she went on. "There is one thing I must say to you both, though. Don't wander about the house in the dark, please. You might fall down the stairs. If you want anything, call out for me and I'll come – but stay in your room. Do you understand me? It's very important. You must stay in your room all night."

CHAPTER TWELVE

Mel sat on the edge of her bed, watching Tom. Mrs Hardacre had shown them into a bare little room, just big enough for the two single beds which were placed side by side. Tom had flopped down on one of them, kicking off his shoes without bothering to undo the laces. And then he had fallen fast asleep. How could he?

Mel might be exhausted, but she wasn't going to let down her guard for a minute. Why was Mrs Hardacre so insistent they should stay in this room? What was she worried they might find? Thoughtfully, Mel fingered the chain around her neck. She'd forgotten about her beautiful pendant. But there it was, snug and warm against her throat. It made her feel brave, and stronger.

She crept over to the door and opened it a

crack. She was determined to take a look around, see what she could discover. It was dark and the stairs looked winding and dangerous, but she wouldn't let that stop her. She was going to find out about Diana Hardacre, see what she was up to. Then Tom would have to listen to her.

Mel stepped out on to the quiet landing. Her palms were sweating and her legs felt unsteady, but she was determined to discover what secrets she could.

And then she heard strange voices, down in the kitchen.

Who was Mrs Hardacre talking to? Had someone come to the house? Was it someone who was looking for them?

Mel felt like rushing downstairs at once and flinging open the kitchen door to shout for help. But then she stopped herself. This other person might be an accomplice of Mrs Hardacre's. They might be cooking up some plan together.

She started creeping as silently as she could down the stairs. It was dark and the old wooden steps were steep and uneven, so she had to go slowly. Her heart in her mouth, she groaned inside at every creak of the boards beneath her feet. Surely she would be heard! Her courage almost failed her, but she forced her trembling legs to go on.

Down, down to the room where her enemy was waiting. Like a spider at the heart of its web.

At the bottom of the stairs, Mel paused for one last rub of the chain to give her luck. Then she tucked it under her sweatshirt and tiptoed on down the shadowy passageway. The voices rose for a few seconds, becoming stronger and louder. And then there was silence.

Mel flattened herself against the wall. Her heart was beating so loudly she felt certain it would give her away. How could she summon up the courage to go on? Because you have to, said a voice inside her. It might be the only chance you'll get.

The kitchen door was ajar. Mel crept up to it, and steeled herself to peep through.

And then she nearly jumped out of her skin.

Mrs Hardacre was sitting at the kitchen table. And she was alone.

Her eyes were shut, and she was holding something in her hands. To her horror, Mel recognised her own hairband. It was a big bright scrunchy one. She must have left it in the kitchen when she was brushing her hair.

Mrs Hardacre began to chant. Softly at first, then louder. She clutched the hairband tightly, swaying back and forth a little.

And then other voices joined in. They seemed to swell from every corner of the room, rising and falling together. Murmuring and muttering, though Mel couldn't make out the words.

She had heard that sound before, though, and the memory of it made her blood run cold.

The voices from the forest! Mrs Hardacre was summoning them up.

To get her!

Mrs Hardacre looked up suddenly, and their eyes met.

CHAPTER THIRTEEN

For a second or two, Mel was frozen in shock. Then she stumbled backwards, gasping, "No!"

Mrs Hardacre rose from the table. "What are you doing?" she snarled.

Mel groped blindly behind her, searching for the solid wall at her back. One hand dragging along the passage wall to guide and support her, she half ran, half staggered for the staircase.

And behind her came Mrs Hardacre.

Mel threw herself up the stairs, sobbing in terror. There was no point now in trying to keep quiet. The only thing on her mind was to get back to Tom as quickly as she could. *If* she could.

"Stop, child!" Mrs Hardacre called. "Come back here!"

But Mel rushed on, panic-stricken. She could hear the pounding footsteps behind her getting closer and closer, gaining on her. Harsh breaths tore at her chest, and the pendant swung wildly to and fro beneath her top.

And then disaster struck. A long black streak shot out of the shadows, and Mel crashed to the ground with a heavy thump. The cat, McCavity, turned to spit at her, its yellow eyes narrowed, before melting back into the darkness.

Mel staggered to her feet, hauling herself up with a desperate arm flung out to grab the bannister. The rickety wooden rails shook, but they held firm. A few paces behind, Mrs Hardacre was stretching out her hand. Those long fingers reached towards her, grasping, grabbing.

With a last frantic bound, Mel burst through the door to their bedroom and slammed it behind her, all her weight against it.

Diana Hardacre rattled the catch. "Let me talk to you!" she hissed through the door. "I can explain everything."

Mel had no breath left to reply, even if she'd wanted to. She leaned as hard as she could against the door, bracing her legs. The door shook again.

Tom sat bolt upright on the bed. "What's going on?" he demanded, bleary-eyed.

Mel fought to control her ragged breathing. "Help me," she panted. "Come here and lean against the door."

Tom made his way over to the door, still half asleep, and put his back against it. "But what's happening?" he asked again. "Who's trying to get in?"

Mel just shook her head. There would be time for explanations later.

And then the rattling and the pushing from the other side of the door stopped abruptly. A pause, and the children heard a noise which was even more alarming.

A key was turning in the lock.

They were trapped!

CHAPTER FOURTEEN

"So you were right all along," said Tom. "Mrs Hardacre is out to get us."

"You bet she is," Mel replied. She'd told Tom all about the chanting voices in the kitchen, and being chased up the stairs. She shuddered at the memory of Mrs Hardacre clutching her hairband, and those cold eyes looking straight into hers. That woman could summon up the forces of evil that lurked in the forest and bring them inside! Where she and Tom were waiting like sitting ducks.

"I had no idea," Tom said. "I thought she was kind, looking after hurt animals and all that."

"We don't know what she's doing with them," Mel said suspiciously, "or with those plants and herbs she's got hanging up everywhere. What are they for?"

This time, Tom didn't tell her she was imagining things. "Well, what do you think we should do now?" he asked.

"We've got to get out of here, quickly" Mel replied. "Somehow."

She went over to the door and listened. Everything was quiet. Mrs Hardacre must have gone downstairs – she knew they weren't going anywhere. She was just going to keep them up there until she was ready. Ready to do what? Mel shivered.

Crouching down, she peered through the keyhole. It was blocked. The key was still in it!

"Tom, I think there's something we can do," she told him excitedly. "She's left the key in the lock. If we can poke something through the keyhole, we can maybe make it fall and then hook it under the door. I saw someone doing that on the telly once."

She examined the door. It was old and badly fitting, so there was a wide gap between its base and the floor. Yes! It might work…

"But what can we use to push through?" Tom asked, looking round the bare room.

Mel touched the chain around her neck. She

pulled it up over her head and looked at the short bar of gold hanging from it. "This should be perfect," she said. "I think it's just about the right size."

"Well, let's go for it then," said Tom. "We don't want to hang around. We can unlock the door and then creep down the stairs and out at the front."

"But she's probably still in the kitchen," Mel said. There was no need to ask who 'she' was. "I've got a better idea. Let's wait till she comes upstairs to go to sleep. Then when it's all quiet, we can try to escape."

"What if she's planning to do something to us before then, though?" Tom asked, his eyes wide.

"That's a risk we're just going to have to take," Mel replied.

CHAPTER FIFTEEN

"What are you doing, snooping around here? You're a wicked girl, but I know how to deal with wicked girls. You'll never get out of this house alive!"

Mrs Hardacre bent over Mel's bed, whispering savagely at her. She was so close, Mel could feel the heat of her breath. She lay there on the bed, rigid with terror. Opening her mouth, she tried to scream, but no sound came out. It was as though she were paralysed, unable to move.

Mrs Hardacre was clasping a thick wooden stick in her hand. With one sudden movement, she brought it crashing down on the pillow with a sickening thump.

Inches from Mel's head.

Then she raised the club higher, and swept her arm down to strike again.

Mel screamed and sat bolt upright. She was bathed in sweat. Her pulse was racing and her whole body was shaking. She looked wildly around, but the room was empty. Apart from Tom, who groaned softly in his sleep and turned over. She must have lain on the bed and fallen asleep, despite promising him she'd stay awake for the next few hours.

There was no sign of Mrs Hardacre. And yet there was something else that remained from her dream.

A steady thump, thump, thump.

Footsteps? But they were coming from above her head.

Someone – or something – was upstairs in the attic!

Now don't panic, Mel told herself. Just stay calm. And then she remembered that flash of white she'd glimpsed up at the window under the eaves. How could she have forgotten? So much else had happened since they'd come to this terrible place that it had gone right out of her mind.

She crept over to her brother and shook him by the shoulder. "Tom, wake up!"

Tom sat up from his fitful sleep, immediately awake this time.

"I can hear noises in the attic," Mel told him. "I think there's somebody up there."

"Is it Mrs Hardacre?" he asked, yawning.

"No, I think she's still downstairs," replied Mel. The faint noise of clattering saucepans was drifting up from the kitchen.

"Maybe we should try to leave now," Tom said. "I don't want to hang around if there's some other weirdo up there."

"But it might be someone else who's locked in, like us," Mel said. "We can't just go without finding out."

"You must be joking!" Tom said in disbelief. "You can't go wandering about the house again. Not after what happened last time. And who knows what's up there – it could be anything!"

Mel hesitated. She was torn. Fear at the memory of that white shadow in the window fought against one awful thought: there might be another child trapped in this house.

"I'm going up there," she told her brother. "Wait for me here. I'll come back, I promise."

"You'd better," Tom said.

Mel crept over to the door and crouched down, so that she was level with the lock. Then she took the chain off her neck and poked the short golden length of metal into the keyhole. She pushed gently but firmly against the end of the key, over and over again.

Yes! At last the key fell to the ground. Mel froze against the door, listening for the sound of Mrs Hardacre coming up the stairs. But there was nothing.

She reached under the door with her pendant, and hooked the key back through with it.

"Wish me luck," she whispered to Tom. Very carefully, she unlocked their bedroom door and glided out through it, replacing the key on the other side. She looked up the winding flight of stairs that led to the attic and forced her trembling legs to start climbing.

At last, she was outside the low attic door. There was a key on the outside of it, just as there had been in their bedroom door. She could hear the footsteps inside. Was she brave enough to turn the key in the lock and find out who – or what – was making them?

She turned the key and opened the door…

CHAPTER SIXTEEN

Over at the far side of the attic room, a white shape seemed to be floating against the window. Mel felt for the door behind her. She had to get out of here! But her legs had turned to jelly and she couldn't control them. She opened her mouth to scream, but only a faint croak came out from her dry lips.

And then the apparition spoke. "Who are you?" it said.

The shimmering form came towards her through the shadows. But as she shrank back in horror, it turned from ghost to boy. A pale, thin boy, but a boy all the same – about Tom's age. He had a mop of black hair, and deep brown eyes with dark circles beneath them – almost as though they were bruised. The long white shirt he was wearing flapped against his dark trousers.

"Who are you?" the boy repeated.

"I'm Mel," she answered. "My brother, Tom is with me, downstairs. And what's your name?"

"William," the boy said. "But what are you doing here?"

"We were lost in the wood," Mel answered. "We saw this house and knocked on the door for help. Mrs Hardacre took us in. Then she locked us in the bedroom downstairs, but I managed to get the key."

"I've been locked in this room as well," William said. "I have to get back to my uncle. He'll be so worried about me."

"Our parents must be, too," Mel said bitterly. "How long have you been here?"

"I'm not sure," he replied, sounding vague. "Quite a long time, I think."

Mel was horrified. What did that woman have in mind, keeping the three of them locked away like this? She shuddered.

"We were going to wait until Mrs Hardacre had gone to bed and then try to escape," she told William.

"No! If we wait, it will be too late," William said, sounding quite agitated. "We have to go now. Straight away."

"Do you know how to get to your uncle?" Mel asked him.

"Oh yes," William replied. "He's near here."

So much for not having any neighbours, Mel thought to herself. She hadn't believed Mrs Hardacre at the time. For all she knew, there was probably a telephone downstairs as well.

"Could you take us there, do you think?" she asked William. "Would your uncle be able to help us?"

"Oh yes," William said confidently. "He'll know what to do."

Mel was torn. Their urgent need to get away from the house fought against her fear of going back into that awful forest at night. They had only just got out of it alive; next time they might not be so lucky.

The evil isn't only out there, she answered herself. It's inside this house and all around. You'll just have to face it.

"Are you sure you can find your way in the dark?" she asked William.

"I've got a torch," he replied, rummaging around on the windowsill. Then, he pulled on a pair of boots. "Come on, let's go."

"We have to get down to our room on the next floor," Mel told him. "Then we can meet Tom, and try to sneak out."

The two of them crept to the door of the attic and listened. Everything seemed quiet. Taking William by the hand, Mel led him to the top of the narrow stairs, closing the attic door silently behind her and turning the key again, as though he were still inside.

They made their way down slowly, step by step. William's heavy boots made such a racket on the floorboards. "Shhh!" she mouthed at him urgently.

"Sorry," he whispered back.

At last, they had reached the bottom. Mel opened the bedroom door and William shot through. She caught a glimpse of Tom's startled face from where he was sitting.

Putting the key back on the outside of the door, she had just stepped into the room herself, when disaster struck.

A noise shattered the silence, exploding on to the still night. It was unlike anything Mel had ever heard before. And it made her flesh crawl.

CHAPTER SEVENTEEN

Peering through the crack in the door, Mel saw McCavity, the black cat, glaring at her from outside on the landing. The fur on his back stood up in spikes and his tail was fluffed to twice its size. He yowled again, loudly.

Immediately, Mel pulled the door shut and flattened herself against the wall beside it. There was no time to jump into bed, because she could hear Mrs Hardacre coming out of the kitchen. She put her finger to her mouth as Tom and William stared at her in alarm.

Down below, the footsteps stopped. There was a silence, which seemed to Mel to last for ever. And then a soft call, "Shh, McCavity! Quiet now!" And Mrs Hardacre went back into the kitchen.

Mel let out her breath in a rush. She went

over to the windowsill where Tom was sitting, his eyes like saucers.

"This is William," she explained. "He was upstairs, in the attic. Locked in, like us. His uncle lives quite near by, and he can find the way to his house."

"I've been thinking," Tom said. "Wouldn't it be better to wait until it gets light, and then try to escape? There seems to be a storm brewing up. Look." And he pointed out of the window.

Mel looked outside. A wind had sprung up. The tall trees were tossing this way and that in the darkness, their branches moaning and complaining. She shivered, as all her doubts and fears returned.

"What do you think, William?" she asked. "Wouldn't it make more sense to wait?"

"No!" he replied definitely. "We have to go now, or it will be too late. Look, there's a thick branch of the creeper just below this window. I could see it from my window, but it was too far away to reach from up there. We can climb down it and jump to the ground. Follow me!"

He opened the window. At once, a fierce gust of wind swept in and snatched the thin curtain, almost tearing it from the wall. William looked out into the night, his dark hair blowing back from his face. Then he swung his leg over the sill and disappeared out of sight.

Tom and Mel exchanged anxious looks.

"I don't want to climb down that thing," Tom said. "It doesn't look strong enough to me."

"I'll go first," Mel told him. "You can come down after me. I'll catch you if you slip, I promise. We've got to get out of here, and this may be the best chance we have. William's our only hope. Come on, Tom – trust me! It'll be fine." She hoped she sounded more confident than she felt.

Cautiously, Mel climbed out on to the windowsill. She grasped the thick creeper and began to lower herself down.

"It's fine," she whispered back up to Tom. "There are loads of footholds, and it feels really quite steady."

Slowly, the children started climbing down. William had already landed on the ground and was shining the torch up at them, so they could see where to put their feet.

And then it all went wrong.

There was a rattling noise, and the front door of the house was flung open.

At once, William switched off the torch and flattened himself against the shadowy wall at the side of the porch.

A pool of light streamed out from the open doorway. Through it, Mel saw a familiar figure striding out.

Mrs Hardacre! She was coming to get them!

There was nowhere to run. No way of escape.

This was the end.

CHAPTER EIGHTEEN

Mel buried her face in the damp, glossy leaves of the creeper, though she knew it was useless to try and hide. She and Tom were trapped, stuck against the wall like butterflies on a pin.

She didn't dare look down again. Silently, she reached up and grasped her brother's heel, just to let him know she was there. He looked wordlessly down at her, his face twisted in fear.

And then the chanting began. Mel could hear the hum of sound beneath the furious gusting of the wind, and shuddered. Why does she have to torture us like this? she said to herself. Whatever she's planning, why not just get it over and done with.

The low muttering went on, rising to a crescendo. And then, suddenly, it stopped. Silence. The front door slammed and the wall of the house was plunged back into darkness.

"You can come down now," came a soft voice from below. "She's gone back inside." And William shone the torch beam up to guide their footsteps once more.

Mel and Tom half-fell, half-slithered on trembling legs down to the ground.

"What happened?" Tom asked William. "What was she doing?"

"She came out with some kind of bird under her arm," William told them.

"The owl!" Mel gasped.

"Well, she talked to it for a while and then she threw it up into the air. It flew off into the wood, and she went back inside. She didn't look round once."

"Lucky for us," Mel said thankfully. "I thought we'd really had it this time."

"Well, I'm not waiting to see if she comes back," William said. "I'll go first and you can follow me. We must hurry!"

And he set off towards the dark forest.

It was hard work keeping up with William: he walked quickly, sometimes breaking into a run. He didn't look round to check that Mel and

Tom were behind him, but forged straight ahead. They were following a path, though Mel couldn't tell if it was the same one that had brought them to the house. She seemed to have lost all sense of direction. She kept her eyes fixed on William's white shirt, flitting through the trees ahead, not daring to look right or left.

They seemed to be all on their own in this part of the wood. The furious wind was still blowing, and tree branches thrashed and tossed all around them. Leaves and twigs that had been torn off by the storm swirled up into the air, sucked away by the whirling gusts and carried off into the night.

"What if another branch breaks?" Tom said worriedly, looking upwards. "You might not be able to save me next time."

A low rumble of thunder sounded now and then from somewhere far away, but the rain held off. The wind blew the scudding clouds away and a full moon sailed out from behind them. Its pale light made the shadows of the woodland seem even deeper.

And then William stopped, looking ahead among the trees.

"Are we nearly there?" Mel asked, when she and Tom had caught up with him.

"Yes, I'm sure it's just up here," William replied. "Come on!" And he took Tom's arm to hurry him along.

"Wait for me," Mel called. She didn't want to be left on her own in this frightening place. She hurried after the two boys.

Then, she gave a yelp of pain, and pitched forward into the cold, damp darkness.

CHAPTER NINETEEN

Slowly, Mel came to her senses. She was lying on the damp forest floor, at the foot of a huge tree by the side of the path. She sat up, shaking her head to clear away the stars that were flashing around it. Her ankle was hurting, and her left foot seemed to be trapped. Reaching down, she discovered it was caught under a thick root. That must have been what had sent her flying.

Gently, she wiggled her foot back and forth. Little by little, she managed to ease it out. The next step was to try and stand up. Grasping the ivy-covered trunk, she hauled herself upright. Ouch! The pain shot up from her ankle. But she could manage to walk if she put most of the weight on her right leg.

There was one problem, though. William and Tom were nowhere to be seen.

What had happened to them? Mel couldn't believe they would just have left her behind, all alone in the middle of the forest. She didn't know which way to turn.

"Tom!" she screamed, into the night. "Where are you? Don't leave me here!"

She whirled around, staring into the storm-tossed night. And the trees stared back at her. The wind shrieked through them, making their branches bend and crack under its force.

But underneath the racket, she thought she heard something even more frightening.

A low rumble, rising through the trees.

Those evil, menacing voices had found her. They had come for her!

Mel staggered against the massive tree, leaning against its sturdy trunk to support herself. She raised both hands to the chain around her neck, grasping it tightly. In her panic, it was all she could think of to do. The storm was swirling around her now. She was a still point at the centre of it, unable to move.

The fury of sound washed over Mel as she clutched the chain. Bolts of sound were flung at her, ringing inside her head until she thought it must explode. She felt as though she was going mad.

She began to shout for help, though her voice could scarcely be heard. And there was no one around to hear her. Thunder was rumbling now, and jagged streaks of lightning threw a stark white light over the wind-tossed trees. As a last resort – and she never knew quite what made her do it – Mel took the pendant out from under her shirt and held it up before her face, as if to shield herself. Grasping it tightly, she prayed desperately for help.

And then she gasped in amazement. A radiant light shone out and the whole chain seemed to come alive in her hands, sparkling with golden light. Its beams fell all around, lighting up the wood as though the sun were shining. Mel could see the path ahead, beckoning her on.

And the noise had stopped. The wind was still blowing, but the muttering, snarling voices had gone. In their place, she heard again that beautiful chorus which had rung out before, when she'd first found the chain. The harmony of deep voices singing sweetly together.

Mel fell back against the tree, sobbing with

relief. Her racing heart began to beat regularly once more, and she looked ahead with new courage. She would find Tom and William, and they would all come through this together. The forest could not beat her!

Finding a stick in the undergrowth to support her left side, Mel began to limp on down the path. She had to get to Tom and William, and make sure they were OK. Had the voices come to them, too?

The wood was strangely quiet now, as though the storm had blown itself out. She shook her broken watch impatiently. If only she knew what time it was! She had no idea how many hours had passed, or whether this terrible night was nearly over.

And then, peering ahead into the darkness, she thought she saw a light ahead. Hope sprang up in her, though she hardly dared trust it. Was her ordeal about to end? Might there be a house there? She limped nearer, her heart in her mouth, praying under her breath. Just let this be William's uncle's place and I'll never do anything bad again, she said to herself. I'll be nice to Tom all the time and I'll never moan about him, ever again. Only please, let us get out of here.

Yes! she cheered silently a few moments later. She could have sunk to her knees and kissed the ground with relief. Standing there before her was a cottage. One of the brightest, most cheerful little houses she had ever seen. It was in the centre of a clearing in the wood, surrounded by a low white picket fence. Behind it, Mel could just make out the shadow of a larger building that she thought might be a church. Perhaps this was where the vicar lived, or even the verger.

Whoever it was, they must be a keen gardener. The light which streamed out of the windows showed a tidy front lawn and beds full of flowers, their glossy heads packed closely together. A big bushy honeysuckle twined its way around the front door. Its sweet scent wafted over to her.

Mel savoured the moment, staring at the charming house. It had pale, roughly plastered walls and a low tiled roof. Smoke drifted its way out of the chimney and off into the night. Like a child's drawing, there were two large windows on the ground floor, one on either side of the door. And in one of them, sat William and Tom.

The two boys were watching a flickering screen. Mel didn't know whether she wanted to throw her arms around Tom or strangle him. So much for brotherly love! He'd left her there in the forest, all on her own. He hadn't even bothered to go back and look for her! Now she knew they were safe, Mel was suddenly furious. How could Tom treat her like this when they'd been through so much together!

She hobbled up the path, lifted the brass knocker and rapped on the door. After a short pause, she could hear the sound of approaching footsteps. The door was flung open, and Mel found herself looking into a kindly face. This had to be William's uncle. They looked so similar. The same dark hair, though his was streaked with grey. He was smiling down at her.

"You must be Mel," he said. "We were just about to come out and look for you."

She looked up and smiled back. Everything was going to be fine!

CHAPTER TWENTY

"Come in, my dear," said the man. "I'm William's uncle, Hadrian. Come through. Tom and William are in the sitting room."

Mel followed him down the short hall. She felt weak with the relief of being safely inside, out of the forest. And then she felt dizzy with anger as she saw Tom, watching television as though he hadn't a care in the world.

"Hello, Tom," she said. "Thanks for coming back for me. I twisted my ankle, by the way, in case you were wondering what happened."

"Tom! It's your sister," said William's uncle, in a slightly sharper tone of voice than before. Tom was just sitting staring at the television.

"Oh, hello, Mel," he said, looking up uninterestedly. "There you are. We couldn't think how you'd got left behind."

"I don't suppose the idea of turning back and looking for me crossed your minds, did it?" asked Mel, trying to keep her voice calm.

The two boys just stared at her blankly for a few seconds.

"Sorry, Mel," Tom said at last. "But you're here now, aren't you? So everything worked out all right in the end."

"No thanks to you!" Mel exploded. But Tom's eyes had gone back to the television screen, and it was clear she wasn't going to get anything more out of him. Some cartoon was on, and they had always been his favourite.

"Oh well, that's boys for you," said William's uncle, rubbing his hands together awkwardly. He was embarrassed by their lack of concern, Mel could tell. "I was just letting them have a little rest before we set off to look for you. I didn't want to leave them here alone. But here you are, which is wonderful. Now, let's go to the kitchen and I'll make you a hot drink. William's told me some of what's been happening to you, but I'd like to hear what you have to say."

Mel followed him through to a snug kitchen at the back of the house. She collapsed into a chair, exhausted. Where to begin? But she felt she could tell this man anything, and once she started to speak, it all poured out. How they'd come across Mrs Hardacre's house and gone inside, what she'd seen and heard down in the kitchen, and how Mrs Hardacre had locked them in their room. She described finding William, and their escape into the forest. And then she told him about twisting her ankle, the storm in the woods, and how she'd managed to limp to the cottage.

The only thing she didn't mention was her chain. For some reason, she felt this should be her secret. No one else needed to know about it, or what it could do. Not even Tom.

"Well, what a time you've had!" said William's uncle. "You've been very brave indeed. I don't know how to thank you for rescuing William from that awful woman and bringing him back to me. I've been beside myself with worry."

"All I want now is for Tom and me to get back to our parents," Mel said, sipping the steaming mug of cocoa which had appeared in front of her. "Please could you ring the police? Or drive us to a police station?"

"Now that might be difficult," said Uncle Hadrian. "I've been trying to ring the police ever since Tom and William turned up here, but the lines are down. I think the storm must have brought down a tree or something. And I'm afraid to say I don't drive. But I can make you comfortable here, and I'll keep trying to get through. I'm sure it will be fixed soon."

Oh well, Mel thought. We've waited long enough. Another hour or so won't make much difference. She yawned and rubbed her eyes.

"Let me show you upstairs to the guest room," said Uncle Hadrian. "You might as well rest until help arrives. At least you should prop that ankle up. Can you manage the stairs?"

"Yes, I think so," said Mel. She followed him up to a small bedroom on the first floor. Its ceiling was low, and the walls were hung with flower-patterned wallpaper. In the corner, a bed piled high with cushions and a thick, downy duvet beckoned her.

Gratefully, Mel sank on to it and closed her eyes. But there was one niggling little thought worrying away at her. She pushed it to the back of her mind. Now it was time to sleep.

CHAPTER TWENTY-ONE

Mel tossed and turned in the wonderfully soft bed. Her body wanted desperately to sleep, but her brain wasn't having any of it. Wake up, it was telling her. Wake up and think. In the end, Mel groaned and sat up, pushing the hair out of her eyes. Her head felt muggy and thick. What was it that had been bothering her since she arrived here? She'd noticed something strange but she'd pushed it to the back of her mind. So what was it? It had struck her as soon as she saw the cottage.

Mel cast her mind back and pictured herself standing there. The curtains were pulled back, light was streaming on the garden and the honeysuckle.

The honeysuckle. That was it! What was honeysuckle doing in bloom now, in early autumn? And how could the garden be so full of flowers at the end of October? Usually there were only a few late roses left by the time her birthday came around.

Mel got up and peered out of the window. She couldn't see anything outside at all, just blank darkness.

There must be some explanation for this, she thought. But, try as she might, she couldn't come up with one. She forced herself to think over everything she'd noticed about the house.

And then she sat bolt upright, wide awake and terrified.

When she was looking at the front of the house, she'd seen only two windows. There was just a ground floor, with a couple of large windows that reached up, nearly to the roof. So what was she doing upstairs now, looking out of a window that didn't exist?

And what about the picturesque chimney, with smoke billowing out of it? There was no fire in the cottage, she was certain of that. She certainly hadn't seen one in the sitting room or the kitchen.

And what about William and Tom watching

television? Since when had kids' cartoons been on in the middle of the night? It didn't make sense to Mel at all.

There was something wrong with this whole house. It was too perfect – as though someone had decided to create a country cottage but had got some of the details wrong. It was just an illusion. There was nothing real behind it.

So what did that say about Uncle Hadrian? How could he possibly have conjured up all of this? And why?

Mel remembered Tom's blank face as he'd looked up from the television screen. Now his lack of interest in what had happened to her seemed sinister. He wouldn't just have left her in the forest, surely. At the time, she'd thought he didn't care. But there had to be some other explanation. She knew Tom. He would never have abandoned her like that unless he had been forced to. She felt ashamed for doubting him.

So where was Tom now?

Mel got up and went over to the door. She could still hear the television's friendly hum. If she could just talk to Tom, ask him a few more questions…Slowly she started down the stairs, her ears and eyes alert. As she reached the bottom, a tall figure loomed up in front of her.

"Why, hello, Mel!" said Uncle Hadrian. "Is everything all right? I've just been trying the phone again, but no luck yet, I'm afraid."

"Um, I was just wondering where Tom was," Mel said. It was the first thing that came into her head. Whatever happened, she mustn't let Uncle Hadrian know she suspected him. "I wanted to make sure he wasn't doing anything he shouldn't be."

"Well, what a good big sister you are," said Uncle Hadrian. "He and William have fallen asleep in front of the television. I think it would be better not to disturb them, don't you? I checked up on them just now and they looked very peaceful."

"Oh, fine," said Mel. What else could she say? Hadrian was standing firmly in front of the door. She couldn't push him aside and march in.

He smiled at her. "And is there anything *you* would like?" he asked kindly. "A glass of water, perhaps?"

"Oh, yes please," muttered Mel, not knowing where to look.

"Come into the kitchen and I'll get it for you," he said. "Then you can go back upstairs and settle down. The phone's going to be fixed any minute now, I'm sure."

He waited for Mel to lead the way into the kitchen, following close behind her. Then he fetched Mel her water and watched as she made her way back upstairs. She was feeling slightly stupid. Hadrian was so calm and friendly, it was hard to believe anything could be wrong. Was her imagination running away with her?

Mel sat on the bed, thinking it all over. Maybe there *was* some winter-flowering honeysuckle that would be in blossom now. Maybe she'd just been mistaken about the windows. Maybe some other room in the cottage she hadn't yet come across had a fireplace in it. Maybe there was a late-night cartoon special she hadn't heard about. And maybe Tom *was* just being thoughtless, leaving her behind in the forest.

But somehow it just didn't add up. She knew there was something seriously wrong.

CHAPTER TWENTY-TWO

Mel sniffed the glass of water suspiciously. She decided not to drink it, just in case anything had been slipped in to make sure she'd fall asleep. She'd wait for a bit in her room, and then go and take another look downstairs. She *had* to find Tom and see for herself he was OK.

After a little while, she opened the door and quietly stepped on to the staircase. She was terrified of running into Uncle Hadrian again. What could she say this time? And would he believe her.

Luckily, it all seemed to be quiet. Mel made her way downstairs and looked around. The kitchen door stood open, and she could see the room was empty. Perhaps she should just take a look around and see if there were any clues as to what was going on. Stealthily, she crept in.

It looked normal enough – a cosy cottage kitchen with a stone-flagged floor, scrubbed pine table and chairs. There was a big vase of flowers in the middle of the table, and Mel absent-mindedly sniffed them.

She recoiled in horror.

An overpowering stench rose up from the beautiful blooms. They stank of decay, and mould, and death. The smell made her head spin and she sank down on to a chair, fighting waves of sickness. Her heart was pounding.

All her doubts came rushing back, and now she was forced to admit they must be true. What was this awful place they'd ended up in? She'd thought at first they were finally safe. The bitter truth was they were in as much danger as they'd ever been. Maybe more.

Where was Tom? Now, she had to find him.

She went out of the kitchen as silently as she could, and made her way towards the sitting room. She had no idea what she could possibly say to Hadrian, should she meet him again, but she had to get to Tom. What had that man done, to make her lively brother so dull and vacant?

The sitting room door was open just a crack,

and she put her eye up to it. She could hardly see anything, so she pushed the door open a little wider.

The sight which met her eyes sent panic spinning through her whole body.

William was standing in the middle of the room. Sitting opposite him on a high-backed chair was Uncle Hadrian. Tom was slumped on the floor at his feet.

"Where is it?" Hadrian was saying in a low, but forceful voice. "I ordered you to find it and bring it back to me."

"I – I don't know," William stammered. "I couldn't see it anywhere."

"So why did you come back without it?" snarled Hadrian. Mel couldn't believe the change in his voice. Gone was the comforting, friendly tone. Now it was cold and brutal.

"You called me! I knew I had to come tonight," said William. He sounded terrified.

"I didn't want you back here empty-handed!" Hadrian barked. "Don't you remember the rhyme? I've told it to you enough times. Say it to me now!"

In a faltering voice, William began to recite:

"A child will make whole what was torn apart,
The cross will be found, by the pure in heart.
On All Hallow's Eve, 'ere the close of night,
That power will shine out, long hidden from
sight."

"Well?" Hadrian snarled at him. "After
everything I've taught you, you must be the
one! I must have the Coldharbour Cross! Then
this forest shall be under my power for ever!"

His voice had risen to a shout. He's given up
playing the cosy uncle, Mel thought. And what's
he done to Tom?

As if to answer her, Hadrian suddenly seized
Tom with one hand, lifting him right off the
floor. "Are you the one I should be sending out
there in search of it?" he hissed.

He stared intently into Tom's dull eyes. "No,
it can't be. I can see nothing inside your head.
I might as well get rid of you now." And he
shook Tom back and forth, like a cat playing
with a mouse before finally killing it.

At the sight, Mel was overcome with fury.
Fear melted in the heat of her anger, and she
flung open the door.

"Put him down!" she shouted. "Now!"

CHAPTER TWENTY-THREE

Hadrian stared at Mel. A cruel smile spread over his face as he dropped Tom carelessly on the floor.

"Well, well," he sneered. "Isn't that sweet! The big sister sticking up for her brother. So what are you going to do about it? Tell your mummy?" And he laughed mockingly.

"You can't treat us like this!" Mel screamed. She rushed forward, lashing out at him furiously without any idea where her blows were falling.

Hadrian held her carelessly at arm's length. "I can treat you any way I want," he said ruthlessly. "I have powers you can't begin to imagine. When I get the cross – and I will – my hold over this forest will be absolute. Then, I won't have to bother with irritating children any more. Or silly little tricks, like dreaming up this house."

Mel twisted out of his grasp. "So what makes you think you're going to get the cross?" she flung back at him. "You haven't found it yet, have you? And the night must be nearly over. William and Tom aren't going to help you, not in the state they're in."

She glanced down at Tom, lying in a pathetic huddle on the floor. Hold on, she urged him silently. I'll get us out of this. Though she had no idea how.

"But I always get what I want," Hadrian said. "And there's one other child here, isn't there? You! Are you going to be my little helper?" He advanced towards her, his mad eyes gleaming.

Frantically, Mel felt behind her back for the door handle. She had to get out of here!

"Oh, don't think you can run away, my dear," Hadrian said softly, but menacingly. "You won't get very far." His eyes bored into Mel's and she felt herself paralysed, unable to move a muscle. She was caught, like a rabbit in the glare of a car's headlights.

Hadrian lunged forward and grabbed her firmly by both arms. Mel allowed herself to go limp in his grasp. "That's better," he said approvingly. "We might as well work together. When we find the cross, we can share the power it brings. How would you like to rule this forest with me?"

"No!" screamed Mel suddenly. She twisted sharply away from him and stumbled out of the room. Hadrian's footsteps were close behind her as she reached the front door of the cottage. She flung herself out of it and limped as fast as she could down the path, towards the gate.

Behind her, the footsteps came to a halt. Mocking laughter rang out into the night. "You can run, but you can't hide!" Hadrian screamed. "Watch this!"

Mel turned back to look. He flung forward his arm, and a jagged fork of lightning shot out from it. Cutting through the sky, its light revealed a huge wall in front of her, stretching up into the night sky. It seemed to be made of glass, or some other transparent, glistening material. And it ran all the way around the edge of the clearing.

"See?" jeered Hadrian. "You can't escape. You're mine now. You will find the cross for me, or…you will never leave this place alive!"

CHAPTER TWENTY-FOUR

Mel stared around hysterically. Hadrian was coming down the path towards her, and a mutter of menacing, snarling voices came with him. Where could she turn? She couldn't stand and wait for him to take her.

The cottage seemed to be shimmering, as though it were dissolving in a heat haze. I've stopped believing in it, Mel thought to herself. It can't exist any more. But she knew the power of her mind alone was not enough to protect her from Hadrian's evil enchantment.

The chain! It had helped her before - maybe it would again. She grasped it firmly, feeling its solid warmth. On an impulse, she snatched it off her neck and held it looped over one hand. Then she started to run, as best she could with her swollen ankle, in a wide circle. She made her way around the glistening barrier that closed them in and towards the dark looming building she'd noticed behind the cottage. Perhaps there might be somewhere inside it she could hide.

Following behind her came Uncle Hadrian. "That's right, my pretty," he called into the darkness. "On you go, into your burrow like a good little rabbit. The big bad fox will get you then for sure!" And he laughed – a menacing, chilling sound.

The voices swirled around him, rising and falling, sending terror shooting into Mel's heart. They were the same voices which had risen to a crescendo in the forest. Now they were back, in the company of their master. Little crackling flashes of lightning came from his fingers and sparked around Mel as she ran.

As her stumbling feet brought her closer to the building, she could see it was in ruins. The outer walls were open to the sky, and there were stars where once a roof had been. It must have been magnificent once – a huge hall, or cathedral even. Inside the structure, large blocks of stone were piled here and there. Any other time, Mel would have loved to explore. But now her eyes just searched desperately for somewhere to hide. The voices clashed harshly at her heels. Hadrian would surely catch up with her at any moment.

A large stone slab over by the end wall caught her attention. Perhaps she could squeeze behind it. Anything was worth a try. Mel ran on, right up to the great boulder. As she reached it, she saw it was in the form of a huge table, pushed right up against the wall. She couldn't hide behind it, and she'd be cornered if she hid underneath. Perhaps she could climb on to it and then up the wall behind? Sobbing with fear, she ran to the table and hauled herself awkwardly up on to its smooth surface. But the wall behind it was steep and sheer. Desperately she scrabbled for foot or hand holds, only to come sliding down again.

There was nothing for it. She turned around, her hands behind her back against the rough stone, and waited for Hadrian to come.

There was nowhere else to run.

CHAPTER TWENTY-FIVE

Hadrian approached Mel, walking slowly now. There was no need for him to hurry – he knew she couldn't escape him. She could see his eyes shining through the dark. The cloud of voices swirled around him – that low, chilling sound which sent terror shooting into Mel's heart.

"So," he called. "Now the chase is over. We have something to find before the night is through? What a lot of time you've wasted."

Mel stared at him in sullen hatred. She clenched her hand tightly around the chain and pressed against the wall behind her with the other, as though to gain comfort from the ancient stone.

And then her searching fingers met something that wasn't stone, but metal. Cold metal. What was it? It seemed to be wedged in between the stones of the wall. She scrabbled urgently behind her back, her eyes never leaving Hadrian's as he advanced towards her. He was nearly at the table now, his arms raised aloft. Lightning crackled lazily around his hands, and the voices which surrounded him were rising in volume. Chanting against her.

She worked away at whatever it was her fingers had found, urgently trying to free it. This might be something she could use as a weapon. From what she could make out, it was a large, flat piece of metal in an ornate shape.

And then with one last pull, she had it. She slowly brought her hand round in front of her.

In her palm lay the most beautiful thing she had ever seen.

It was a heavy golden cross, covered with tiny, intricate pictures and patterns. Mel had no time to examine them closely, but she couldn't miss the huge sparkling blue stone set in its heart. The four arms stretched out from this beautiful, magnificent centre.

Then Mel gasped in wonder. One arm of the cross was shorter than the other three, as though it had been snapped off. And she knew exactly where the missing piece was – at the centre of the chain in her other hand!

Fumbling, clumsy, she fitted the two jagged ends together. They slid into each other so seamlessly, it was impossible to see the join. There must have been some hidden catch, for there they stayed, so that the cross was perfect, swinging from its ornate chain.

Mel stood tall and proud, facing Hadrian as his arm stretched up for her. She raised one arm high, with the cross grasped firmly in it. Frowning with concentration, she sent all her hopes and prayers into its shimmering, glowing centre. She thought of Tom, lying helpless in the spellbound cottage; her parents, searching for them, her grandmother, and the wisdom she'd tried to pass on. She thought of her home, and the people she loved.

The wonderful cross glowed and pulsated with light. It pierced the darkness of that gloomy place and sent the shadows flying.

"The cross!" shrieked Hadrian. "It belongs to me! It shall be mine!"

And with one bound, he leapt up on to the stone table. Right where Mel was standing.

CHAPTER TWENTY-SIX

Hadrian towered over Mel, his eyes alight with greed and desire. He stretched out a hand for the cross, which she was holding up in the air. For a second or so, they grappled together on the stone slab.

Then, Hadrian grasped the chain. At once, he let out a howl of anguish. A blue flame ran up his arm and swallowed up his whole body. His tall frame was outlined in fire. Then, staggering back, he fell from the stone slab and collapsed on the ground. The clearing was filled with sound, as the muttering, menacing chorus of voices rose up into the air. Now they took shape as a swarm of black shadows, swirling around his head before shooting up, up, up into the sky.

And when Mel looked down again, the cross's shimmering light showed nothing on the ground but a scorched patch of grass.

Then she held her breath in wonder as her ear caught a few faint notes swelling up around her. It was that haunting chorus she'd first heard when she'd found the chain. Deep voices, singing solemnly together, rose up from the cross and filled the air with sweetness. Tears came to her eyes, spilling on to her cheeks.

She looked around in amazement as the ruin in which she stood came to life. This is what it must have looked like centuries before. The crumbling walls were now complete, stretching far above to a vaulted roof. Magnificent arched windows were set along them, and the room was filled with long tables and men dressed in brown robes seated at these tables, while the singing voices rose to a powerful crescendo.

As the last haunting echo died away, the vision disappeared. She was standing in a ruin once more. And stumbling towards her, through the darkness were William and Tom.

Carefully, Mel put the cross around her neck and ran to meet them. She hugged Tom close to her, lost for words. The two boys were dazed and frightened, but other than that they seemed fine.

"What's happened?" Tom said.

"What are we doing out here?" William added. He didn't mention his uncle.

Mel looked beyond them to where the cottage had stood. In its place, all she could see were a few boulders scattered here and there on the grass. The picket fence, the flowers, the plastered walls and tiled roof had all gone. Vanished into thin air, along with the evil genius who had created them.

She looked into the forest beyond. The transparent walls thrown up by Hadrian around the clearing had disappeared. They were free to go. Somewhere deep in the wood, a bird was singing. The first faint flush of dawn tinged the sky. All Hallow's Eve was over.

"Come on," she said to the boys. "I'll explain it all later. Now I think we can finally get out of this place."

She put an arm around each of them and turned in what she hoped was the right direction.

"Oh, don't go just yet," said a voice.

It was Mrs Hardacre.

CHAPTER TWENTY-SEVEN

"Get away from us!" Mel screamed, tearing the cross off her neck and holding it up to shield them. She was exhausted and desperate. After all they'd been through – to be caught again, when they'd so nearly escaped! It was an unbearable thought.

"You don't need to be afraid," Mrs Hardacre said. "I'm not going to hurt you." She spread wide her arms to show she meant no harm, and took a step backwards.

Holding the cross, Mel felt stronger and able to stand up to her. "Oh yes?" she said. "So why did you lock us up? What were you going to do to us?"

She didn't believe the woman for a second. It was all very well to say she meant them no harm, but Mel couldn't forget how they'd suffered in that house. She'd been terrified. Scared out of her wits.

She glared at Mrs Hardacre, but her expression soon changed to one of surprise. What was going on? William had run out from behind her and thrown his arms around the woman, hugging her tightly round the waist. She looked down at him, and an expression of real tenderness lit up her pale face. Mel stared at the two of them in disbelief.

"I was only trying to protect you," Mrs Hardacre said, lifting her dark eyes to Mel. "I couldn't let you wander about in the forest on All Hallow's Eve. Not knowing what I knew."

"Well, why did you keep William locked up in the attic, too?" Mel asked suspiciously.

"William is my son," Mrs Hardacre replied simply. "Hadrian had taken him and turned the boy's mind against me. His own mother! He didn't even recognise me. I had rescued him and brought him home. I was doing my best to heal him, but I knew Hadrian wanted him back and his call would be hard to resist. So I tried to keep William locked in with me for his own safety. At least until All Hallow's Eve was over."

"But I helped him escape," Mel said, almost to herself. "And he took us straight to Hadrian."

"You were not to know," replied Mrs Hardacre, smiling. "And in the end, it was best that you did come here. You found the cross, didn't you? I couldn't reach you, but I saw."

Above her head, a dark shape swooped through the sky to land in a nearby tree. It was an owl, with one injured foot. He watched them intently through huge golden eyes, then settled down to sleep away the new day.

"Why didn't you tell me all this?" Mel asked her. "When we were in your house?" And a horrible image flashed into her mind – Mrs Hardacre, holding the hairband and chanting, while those voices swirled in the air. Could she really trust her?

"You wouldn't have believed me, would you?" Mrs Hardacre said. "Perhaps I was wrong, but I thought I could protect you and keep you safe. There are forces of evil in this forest, but I have some power to resist them. When you saw me in the kitchen, I was trying to help you and increase your own strength. For you are strong in spirit, Mel. You are a special child."

Mel looked into the woman's pale face and deep-set eyes. Was she telling the truth? And as she gazed, another thought struck her. Who did that face remind her of?

"William is your son," she said, "that means, Hadrian is…"

"Yes," replied Mrs Hardacre. "That means, Hadrian is my brother."

Mel stared at her in horror. How could she possibly believe a word the woman said? Was it not just as likely that she and her brother were in league together? He was rotten and wicked, so why should Mrs Hardacre be any different?

She took a step backwards, fear showing plainly on her face.

Mrs Hardacre grasped her arm with a grip like iron. "Wait!" she said. "I can explain. Both Hadrian and I were trained in the ancient art of magic as children." Mrs Hardacre went on. "I have tried to use the knowledge I gained in healing, but he…"

Her voice trailed away and she looked sadly at Mel. "Well, you have seen what he became. He wanted power, and this forest is a dangerous place for such ambition."

"So how do I know you don't want it, too?" Mel asked her suspiciously.

"Nothing I say can persuade you, but I know you will recognise the truth," said Mrs Hardacre simply. "After all, you have found the cross, and fulfilled the prophecy."

"I don't understand anything," Mel said despairingly. "I don't know how we got lost in the first place, or why no one seems to be looking for us, or why this wood is such a terrible place."

"No one is looking for you, because no one knows you are lost," said Mrs Hardacre. "You have entered this wood in another dimension. That is how you found my house, which does not exist in the forest you know. Because it is All Hallow's Eve, and you are the girl you are, you have slipped from one world to another. And brought your brother with you." She smiled at Tom, who was sitting on the ground, his back against a large boulder, yawning and rubbing his eyes. He still looked half asleep.

"There has been evil in this wood for many years," she went on. "Centuries before, there was a monastery here, but it was torn down by violent men. The monks were killed or forced to run for their lives through the forest. None survived."

Mel was horrified, remembering those sweet solemn voices she'd heard singing together. "I found the chain in a hollow tree trunk," she said to Mrs Hardacre. "I suppose one of them must have hidden it there."

"Where it has waited all these years for you to find it," said Mrs Hardacre. "The abbot's holy cross and chain are all that remain of the monastery. Hadrian knew they were destined to be found and the cross made whole once more. He believed it would make his power complete, so he could rule over this wood for ever. But in the end, the cross just reflected back his own evil ambition and greed. Only when it is in the hands of a pure and loving spirit, can its force be unleashed. And Hadrian should have known it could never be used for wicked ends."

Mel looked down at the shining gold cross in her hand, with the huge sapphire sparkling at its centre. She gazed more closely at the engraving with which it was covered: suns, moons and stars, serpents twining their way along each arm, and flames licking around them. It was very beautiful, and so powerful.

"And now the ghosts in this wood have all been laid to rest," said Mrs Hardacre softly. "I know I shall mourn for my poor brother, but perhaps he is finally at peace. I said farewell to him many years ago. You have healed my house, and brought my son back to me."

Mel met her gaze, and saw the kindness of spirit shining out of it. Finally, she knew whom she could trust. "I'm sorry I doubted you," she said. "I didn't know who to turn to, and there was so much I couldn't understand. I'm only glad it's all over now. Will you keep the cross here, in the forest? It's where it belongs."

And she held up the magnificent golden pendant one last time. The two of them watched its rays shine out in the pale dawn light, marvelling at their beauty.

Then, Mel pressed the cross into Mrs Hardacre's hands. "We have to go," she said. "This is your world, and we have to find ours again now." She felt tired and empty, but completely at peace with herself. She had done what she was meant to do, and she and Tom were safe. Now they could go home.

"I know," said Mrs Hardacre. "Just take any path out of this clearing and you will find your way safely back. Don't worry – you will find no time at all has passed. But first, I shall wipe your brother's mind clean. He must remember nothing of this."

She took Tom's face in her hands, gazing into his eyes and speaking quickly in a low tone. Then she joined his hand with Mel's. "*You* will never forget," she said, "but I know you will keep the knowledge safe. Goodbye, my dear, and thank you for everything you have done. Bless you."

Mel stood and watched as William and his mother made their way to the edge of the clearing. They paused for a moment, and Diana Hardacre raised one hand to wave. Then the two small figures disappeared into the forest.

"Come on, Tom," said Mel, setting off at a run down the path. She quite forgot to limp, for there was no need – her ankle was fine. "I'll race you. The car's just up here."

And this time, it was.

Other books in this series:

Ripples of Fear
Ghost Hunting
Lost Souls
A Visit from Beyond
One of our Demons is Missing